Rascal

RACING AGAINST TIME

Collect all of Rascal's adventures:

Rascal

RACING AGAINST TIME

CHRIS COOPER

ILLUSTRATED BY JAMES DE LA RUE

EGMONT

EGMONT

We bring stories to life

First published as *Tramp: Racing Against Time* by Puffin in 2004
This edition first published in Great Britain in 2015
by Egmont UK Limited
The Yellow Building, 1 Nicholas Road, London W11 4AN

ISBN: 978 1 4052 7533 0

58629/1

www.egmont.co.uk

A CIP catalogue record for this title is available from the British Library

Typeset by Avon DataSet Ltd, Bidford on Avon, Warwickshire
Printed and bound in Great Britain by CPI Group

For my mum

CHAPTER 1

Winter had arrived and the days were at their shortest. By the time Rascal saw lights up ahead, it had been dark for a few hours. A small flame of hope sparked inside the dog at the sight of them – perhaps he'd find a place to rest

and shelter from the cold there? But
it was hard to keep that hope alive. As
night had fallen, so had the temperature.
The chill wind buffeted him, and the
occasional flake of snow in the air
hinted at even worse weather on the
way. Pushing through his tiredness,
Rascal continued towards the glow of
the electric lights.

It wasn't easy to be cold and alone like this again. The dog had been forced to delay his long journey several weeks earlier, when his back leg had been fractured by a car. Luckily for Rascal, Judy, a volunteer for the local animal shelter and a true dog lover, had taken him in. He had grown accustomed to being warm and well-fed at her house while his leg mended.

And yet, Rascal hadn't been able to shake the restless feeling at the back of his mind. Judy was a great owner, but she wasn't *his* owner. She was kind and loving to him, but she was that way with all dogs. That's why Judy volunteered to act as a foster owner for any dogs from the shelter that needed special attention. Every time Rascal found himself relaxing and starting to enjoy life with Judy, an image of his old master, Joel – his true master – would pop into his mind, No, he knew he had to continue on his journey home, just as soon as he could.

At last, the day came when Rascal was taken to the vet's and the splint on his leg removed. He touched the floor gingerly with his back paw. It felt good to walk on all fours once again, even if the muscles of the injured leg felt weak through lack of use.

It was time to move on.

Judy was sitting in her favourite chair with the newspaper when Rascal came up to her and pawed her knee.

'You're not looking for more food, are you?' she asked. 'I've never seen a dog eat as much as you did this morning!'

Rascal just looked at this woman who had shown him such kindness. In a rush he leaned forwards and gave her face a lick.

'Get off, you great soppy thing!' laughed Judy.

Rascal wandered out to the garden – out of Judy's line of vision. He looked at the fence ahead of him. He had jumped over this fence once before, but that had been before his back leg had been injured. It might not be so easy now.

Rascal took a breath and charged towards the fence. As before, he sailed over. The instant he landed on the pavement on the other side, he knew that his status had changed. He was not a pet any more. He was a stray dog again, trying to find his way home.

The rest of the day was a blur of sore feet and aching bones and a growing emptiness in his stomach, as Rascal headed west. It didn't take long to leave the town behind him, and then he was crossing open land. A large highway ran straight west, and he kept it in sight as if navigating along the banks of a mighty river.

Knowing that he must find shelter before he could give in to sleep, Rascal

carried on long after the sky had
darkened. And that's when he saw the
lights up ahead . . .

CHAPTER 2

They belonged to a small café, set back from the highway, and a small motel just beyond that.

Rascal could smell the food from a long way away. Although he had eaten as much as he possibly could at Judy's house that morning, he was back to his usual condition – starving. Perhaps he could find something to eat in the rubbish bins round the back of the café?

But, as he neared the building, the front door opened and someone stepped out. He was young and his long hair was pulled back in a loose ponytail. The light jacket he wore wasn't enough to keep out the cold evening air.

The man had a kind, open face and Rascal thought that it was worth a try to see if he had any food. The dog gave a friendly bark.

'Hey, boy,' said the man, rubbing his

hands together to warm them.

Rascal barked again, wagging his tail. Then he sat down expectantly.

The man hesitated, then grinned. 'I get it,' he said. 'It's food you're after, right?'

He opened the plastic container he had been carrying under one arm, and smiled.

'You do realise these leftovers were going to be my lunch for tomorrow?'

He pulled a few strips of bacon out and tossed them to Rascal, who scoffed them down in an instant. They were cold, overdone almost to a crisp, and completely and utterly delicious.

'I guess that's why they call them doggy bags,' laughed the man. He began to walk across the parking lot to the motel that adjoined the café. 'You'd better go home now, doggy,' he said over his shoulder. 'Radio said worse weather's on the way . . .'

Rascal watched as the man entered

one of the rooms on the ground level of the motel. Then the dog took up position outside the café entrance. Maybe he would be just as lucky with the next person who came out? He waited and waited, but no one came.

At last, a face did appear at the café door. It was a woman, but she didn't come out; she just locked the door from the inside, gave Rascal a suspicious look, and then turned round, clicking off the light at the front of the café. There would be no more food tonight.

Rascal turned his attention to finding a place to sleep. The doorway of the café

offered little protection against the wind.
Rascal padded round to the side of the
building. There was a large rubbish
skip here. It wasn't much, but the
narrow gap between it and the wall
offered a little shelter. Wearily, Rascal
crawled in.

It was so cold now that Rascal
could hardly get to sleep.
When he finally did drop
off, his dreams were shot
through with frost
and snow.

It wasn't hard for the sound of a door slamming to pull Rascal from this fitful sleep. He opened his eyes. In the distance, the man from the café, the one who had given him some food, was leaving his motel room. He went along the walkway, pulling change from his pocket, until he reached a vending machine.

Rascal hauled himself out and made his way across the parking lot. The man was heading back to his room when he saw the dog.

'What are you doing still out?' the man asked.

Rascal wagged his tail, but he was too cold and tired to muster much of a bark.

A frown clouded the man's face. 'Haven't you got a home to go to?' he asked.

Rascal took a step closer. Now that he was in the light, the man could have a better look at him.

'I don't think you do,' he murmured thoughtfully. He glanced in the direction of the motel lobby. 'What they don't know won't hurt them,' he said at last. 'Come on.'

Rascal followed him along the walkway. The man unlocked the door to his room and held it open for Rascal. The dog padded into the warmth of the small room. He instantly settled into a corner.

'Just don't bark,' said the man, making sure the curtains were completely drawn so that no one might spot his guest.

Rascal was half asleep when the light was clicked off. Seconds later he heard the sound of bed springs as the man sat up.

'Hey!' hissed a voice from across the room, and Rascal could almost feel its grin in the dark. 'You don't snore, do you?'

CHAPTER 3

Rascal's journey so far had been a long, hard trek. Apart from stops to rest or eat, his entire existence consisted of the exhausting task of just keeping going, of putting one paw in front of the other, hour after hour.

But the next day was different. Rascal travelled in style! After an early and hasty breakfast, the man, who said that his name was Freddie, loaded his one bag into the boot of the little car parked outside. The car had seen better days – its body was mottled with dents and patches of rust. There were stickers across the rear bumper and the bottom of the back window.

Rascal waited patiently and watched the man.

'You sure you haven't got an owner?' asked Freddie at last. Then he shrugged.

'Well, you're not the usual sort

of hitchhiker, but I could use some
company for the rest of the trip,' he said.
He opened the passenger door. 'You
talked me into it!'

Rascal didn't follow much of what
the man was saying, but he knew better
than to turn down an offer like this. He
hopped into the car and settled himself

on the front seat. The floor was covered with sweet wrappers and styrofoam cups.

'Excuse the mess,' said Freddie as he started up the car. And then they were off! Once they had joined the highway, Rascal knew they were going in the right direction because the morning sun lay behind them. Freddie kept a woolly hat pulled over his ears as he drove. He didn't have gloves on, but he'd pulled the sleeves of his sweatshirt down to cover his hands.

'Heater doesn't work too well,' he said to his passenger. 'But the radio does!'

Freddie spent a few minutes searching

for a song he liked. When he found one he turned it up good and loud. Rascal just looked out of the side window as mile after mile slipped by, each one a mile closer to home.

'What should we call you, anyway?' shouted Freddie, looking across at the passenger seat. He noticed that the dog's tail was wagging away. It seemed to be keeping time with the beat of the music from the radio.

'Got it!' exclaimed Freddie. 'We'll call you "Rocker", yeah?'

They drove on. After a while, they stopped to get petrol and Freddie bought snacks for them to eat on the way. He added to the mound of empty packets and wrappers that littered the car's interior.

'Gotta keep an eye on how much I spend,' said Freddie. 'I can't really afford this whole trip, but I just couldn't resist dropping in on my sister and her family for the holidays. It'll freak her out!' He grinned at the thought. 'If we make good time, we should get there later on tonight.'

Rascal was content to let the man chat away to him. Every so often, Freddie would let out a yell of recognition when

they played a favourite of his on the
radio.

It was still early when they stopped
for dinner, though it was already dark.
Freddie bought a burger, which he

shared with Rascal, and a portion of French fries, which he wolfed down himself. There was just time for Freddie to nip to the fast food restaurant's toilets, and for Rascal to go to the patch of wasteland behind the building for the same reason, and then they were back on the road.

As the evening wore on, there was less and less traffic on the road. Despite the cold, Freddie had cracked a side window open to keep the car from fogging up. It began to snow, lightly at first, but then more strongly. The car's windscreen wipers were on, but they only worked from time to time and it was hard to see very far ahead. The screen filled with flakes between each swish of the wipers.

Freddie slowed down. 'Hoped we'd beat the snow,' he muttered, leaning forwards against the steering wheel and peering ahead.

But Rascal had other things on his mind. An odd feeling had crept up on him – slowly at first, but as the minutes and miles went by, he became more and more certain of it.

He was nearing his home!

No human could know how Rascal knew this. It was a unique combination

of smells in the air, smells that only
a dog could identify. Taken together,
they were as recognisable to the dog
as a picture might be to a human ...
With a jolt of excited anticipation,
Rascal realised that he must be no more
than a day's journey from home – less
time than that in a car! He might be
reunited with Joel sooner than he'd ever
imagined!

Rascal could hardly sit still as the

notion gripped him. His long, hard journey across the country might soon be over! He let out a little bark of joy.

'Oh, you like this song, do you?' asked Freddie, reaching for the volume control on the radio. 'Me too! It's an oldie but a goodie.' He turned up the music until they could feel the bass rumbling through their chests, with Freddie singing along to the chorus and Rascal joining in with a bark every so often.

The music was thumping away as they passed a police car parked in the central reservation between the westbound and eastbound lanes of the highway.

The song had finished as they rounded a bend in the road. A DJ on the radio began chattering away. Impatiently, Freddie bent down to find a different station with less talk.

'Jabber, jabber, jabber . . . I say cut the waffle! We need more music and less talk,' he said. 'Right, Rocker?'

But then everything went very, very wrong.

The car hit a patch of ice on the slick surface. The back wheels swung out wide, as if with a mind of their own. Freddie jerked upright, pulling both hands on to the steering wheel again, but it was too late. The car was spinning out of control. Rascal was suddenly aware that the constant background noise of the tyres on the road had become a rumble. The car was bouncing up and down as it sped across rougher terrain. It had left the hard shoulder and was barrelling down the ravine that ran alongside this stretch of the highway.

Rascal just had time to see the trees ahead, stern and silent in the snow, and then there was a terrible sound of metal crumpling and glass shattering as the car struck something, a jolt of pain, and Rascal fell into unconsciousness.

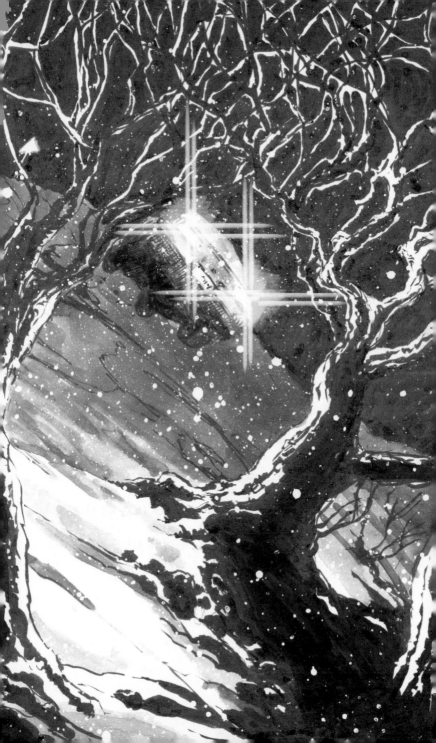

CHAPTER 4

He woke to blackness. The car's engine was silent, but the radio still let out a hiss of static. Urgently, Rascal sniffed at the figure slumped forwards in the driver's seat. Freddie was not moving and Rascal could smell blood, but he could also hear the low rasp of the man's breath.

The side window next to Rascal had smashed as the front end of the car crumpled in on itself. It was difficult in the cramped space, but Rascal managed to turn himself around and wriggle through the gap. Chunks of glass dug into the pads of his front paws, but he ignored them.

Snow was still falling, but not much

had settled on the ground yet. Rascal ran back up the embankment to the highway. Once he reached the hard shoulder, he looked back. Through the swirl of falling snow and in the darkness of the ravine, it was hard to spot the crashed car.

There were no lights visible anywhere, nothing Rascal could do but wait until another vehicle passed by. But it was late by now and the road was empty. He stood trembling in the cold. Part of him wanted to rush back down to the car

and see how Freddie was, but he forced himself to stay at the side of the highway. The falling snow had soon covered the tyre tracks that led off the road.

At last Rascal heard the sound of an approaching car. Moments later headlights appeared.

Rascal went right up to the edge of the hard shoulder and began to bark for all he was worth. The driver just beeped the horn – perhaps to make sure the dog

didn't run out into the highway – and moved the car out into the overtaking lane. As it whizzed past, Rascal began to charge in the same direction, still barking. He glimpsed a pale face in the passenger seat looking back at him, and then the car was gone and all he could see was the red glow of its rear lights in the snow.

The road was deserted again. How long before another car went by? And when it did, why wouldn't it too simply speed by? Rascal didn't know what to do, he –

The police car!

The police car hadn't been far back down the road. Just around the bend, in fact.

Rascal began to trot along the hard shoulder. He hadn't gone far, when he saw a flash of red and blue lights rounding the bend and heading this way. This was even better – the police car was coming to him!

It was going slowly and it stopped altogether when it caught Rascal in the glare of its headlights. A police officer got out on the passenger side.

'There it is, just like the caller said!' he shouted back to the driver, and then to

Rascal, 'Here, boy!'

Rascal knew that he had to lead them to Freddie's car. He let out a short bark.

'COME HERE!' shouted the officer, more impatient this time. 'You're going to cause an accident!'

He walked towards the dog with a torch in his hand, and the car, lights still flashing, crawled along the hard shoulder behind him. Making sure that the man never got close enough to grab him, Rascal trotted ahead.

'Stupid dog,' muttered the police officer irritably.

When he was near the right spot,

Rascal veered off the road. The policeman went to follow him, but then a voice called from inside the police car: 'Let it go! It probably lives on a farm near here. We'll never catch it!'

The first police officer turned back. 'You reckon?' He started back to the car.

No! They were going to leave! But they hadn't seen the crashed car! What about Freddie? Rascal had to do something. Bounding towards the man, he began to bark as loudly and fiercely as he could.

Rascal was not attacking, but in the dark and snow, the policeman didn't

know that.
He brandished
the torch like
a weapon,
while the dog
completed a loop around the man,
jumping and barking like crazy. Then
Rascal headed back off the road.

The other police officer was out of
the car now.

'It's not going to leave, is it?' he called
to his partner. 'We'd better do something
about it before it causes an accident on
the highway.'

They tracked Rascal in the beams of

the torches – 'There it goes! That way!' –
until the beams stopped on the crashed
car.

'We're too late!' snarled one officer.
'There's *already* been an accident!' He
turned and ran back to the police car to
radio for help, while the other went to
Freddie's car.

Rascal stayed back and watched from
the first line of trees. The police officer
crouched at the side of the car, talking
to Freddie in a low voice. Minutes later,
Rascal heard a siren approach and then
an ambulance arrived at the side of the
road.

The dog looked on with concern as the long-haired man was lifted from the car and put on a stretcher by two paramedics. He didn't seem to be awake, but his head was rolling from side to side. He was alive!

The dog was so intent on Freddie's fate that he didn't even notice footsteps behind him. Suddenly a collar looped around his neck.

'You've caused enough trouble for one night,' said the police officer's gruff voice. And then Rascal was being tugged away and there was nothing he could do.

CHAPTER 5

Like most other children in his school, Joel had found it hard to stop his mind from wandering during the last lesson of the day. For most of the children it was because there were only a few more days before the winter holidays, but not

Joel. Christmas had always been Joel's favourite time of year, but he couldn't look forward to it now.

As he sat alone on the school bus home, he leaned his head against the window. A kid in the seat behind him was saying that they'd had snow in the hills not far to the east. The same weatherfront might be moving their way. That meant they might have a white Christmas this year! The bus was filled with excited talk of sledding and snowball fights.

Joel didn't join in. As usual, he was thinking about Rascal. Could he really expect to see the dog again?

A man walking a dog outside caught Joel's eye. He recognised both man and pet immediately. They lived further down Joel's street. He didn't know the man's name, but he was all too familiar with the dog's – Fritz!

The black-and-tan Dobermann had been Rascal's biggest enemy in the neighbourhood. Whenever Joel and Rascal had walked past Fritz's house, the Dobermann would unleash a torrent of savage barks at the smaller dog. Rascal had always responded by pressing himself even closer against Joel's legs.

On those unlucky occasions when they had encountered each other in the dog park – the only spot in the area where dogs were allowed to run off their leads – Fritz went out of his way to chase Rascal.

Joel watched the big dog now as it tugged his owner towards the dog park. The unfairness of it all struck him again. It had been months since he'd had the chance to take Rascal there.

When Joel got home, Mum had already finished work.

'Any emails?' he asked, flinging his school bag aside.

Of course, Mum knew what he was asking about. Ever since they had spotted a dog that looked exactly like Rascal on the news, they had done as much as they could to track him down. Joel's mum and dad had called dozens of animal shelters. They had sent emails to several missing pets websites across the country. Joel's mum had even helped him to set up a website so that people could send information about Rascal.

Mum shook her head. There had been no emails, but it was clear that she was excited about something. 'There was a phone call,' she said, 'from the TV station.'

Joel's heart leapt. 'Has someone found Rascal?' he asked anxiously.

'No,' said Mum, 'but there's a news producer at the station who saw our website. She thinks it's a good story. They want to interview you on the morning news.'

Joel's first reaction was one of nerves – he didn't like talking in front of his class, let alone goodness-knew-how-many TV viewers – but he quickly fought them down. He was willing to do anything that would increase their chances of finding Rascal.

CHAPTER 6

Joel Holland would have been
astonished to know it, but Rascal was no
more than twenty miles away. However,
there wasn't much chance that the
dog would be getting any closer. He
had been brought to an animal shelter

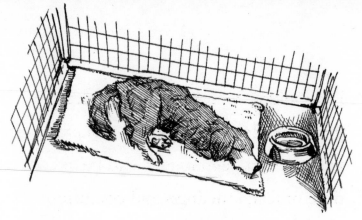

and led along a narrow corridor with enclosures on either side.

Rascal was put into one of these. It was quite comfortable in there – there was a bowl of fresh water and some bedding on the concrete floor for him to sleep on. He did manage to sleep a little, but his dreams now took him back to his earliest memories of puppyhood. He had been in an animal shelter like this when he was very little.

He couldn't remember how he had got there. Even though all the shelter workers had been nice, it had been a time of fear, loneliness and confusion for him. That awful mix of feelings had only ended when the Holland family had come and taken him away from that place. Now he was back in another animal shelter and all those feelings swept back inside him and remained throughout the night.

Daytime came as a relief. As soon as one dog noticed the pale sunlight it let out a bark, and then it seemed as if every other dog in the place joined in. Rascal

could hear and smell all the other dogs –
there seemed to be at least eight of them
– but he was only able to see the one in
the enclosure opposite his, a sad-eyed
Cocker Spaniel.

The day passed slowly. Every time a
shelter worker brought food or fresh
water, they would take the time to chat
to each of the dogs, but there were
still long stretches in which nothing
happened.

Just the sound of the door to their
section opening was enough to set off
a chorus of barks. This happened in
the middle of the morning, and two

women walked between the two rows of enclosures.

'I'm Lisa, the shelter's general manager. And, of course, this is where we keep the dogs, Becca,' the taller woman was saying. 'Don't worry, they won't bark quite so much once they know you,' she added with a laugh. 'Your duties will mostly be in the office, but you might have to help out here sometimes too. It's basically a matter of feeding them, changing their bedding, and making sure they've got water. Common sense, really.'

The other woman, Becca, stopped at

the enclosure opposite Rascal's and bent down to read the card taped to it.

'*Toby, male, eight years old*,' she read aloud. '*Nice temperament.*'

Lisa, nodded. 'We put that information right there for any family who might want to adopt a pet,' she explained. She reached an arm through the door and stroked the Spaniel behind the ear. 'Toby here's a lovely dog – aren't you, Toby? Yes, you are! – but he's quite a bit older than what most families are looking for. You know, people love puppies.' The Spaniel had closed his eyes and angled his head so that Lisa's hand was

scratching the perfect
spot. 'Toby came to
us when his owner
passed away,' continued
Lisa. 'There were no
relatives who could take him
in, so we've been trying to find a home
for him. Haven't we, Toby?'

Becca nodded towards Rascal's
enclosure. His card read: *Not available for
adoption at this time.*

'What about this one?' asked Becca.

'Ah well, this is our new arrival,'
said Lisa.

'So what happens to him?' asked Becca.

'Well, the county vet will look him over later on today,' Lisa replied. 'Once we know he hasn't got rabies or anything nasty like that, we'll be able to clean him up a bit. Then we'll hold him for five days and hope that someone comes and claims him.' She frowned a little. 'I'd be surprised if anyone *did* come and claim him, to be quite honest. I couldn't read his chip, and apparently he was running loose. He caused an accident out on the highway.'

'And what if no one claims him?'

Lisa sighed. 'Well, we do our best to put every unclaimed dog we get in here

up for adoption, however long it takes,'
she said. 'The only time we can't is if
we know a dog's too dangerous to fit
into a new home.' She squatted down
and gave Rascal an appraising look.
'The report said that this one might be
a biter. Of course, it could just be that
he was reacting untypically in a stressful
situation. But we'll have to keep an eye
on him.'

Lisa got to her feet. 'If a dog doesn't
have the right temperament to be
placed in a home, we'll still try and keep
them here as long as we can. It's only
when the place is full up and another

dog arrives that we have to face hard decisions about what to do. That's our worst-case scenario – having to have a dog put down because we're out of space. It doesn't happen often, thank goodness, but that's the absolute worst part of the job. That's why we're going to expand the shelter in the spring – we'll be able to house lots more strays then.'

'But . . . the shelter's full up right now, isn't it?' asked Becca.

'Almost.' A cloud of worry crossed Lisa's face. 'That's why we'll have to keep our fingers crossed that we don't get any more new arrivals for a while.'

CHAPTER 7

Rascal was well-fed and comfortable
enough at the shelter. The workers there
were kind – it was clear that they loved
animals – but they were too busy to
devote a lot of time to any one dog. The
time crept by slowly.

The best part of the day was when
he was let out into the dog run outside.
Lisa or one of the other shelter workers
would pull a rope that raised a gate at
the back of Rascal's enclosure out to
one of two big runs outside. It was a
chance to stretch his legs and breathe in
fresh air again. The runs were enclosed
by a tall, wire-mesh fence, beyond

which Rascal could see the road leading towards the hills to their west.

A little snow had settled on the ground, and it was too cold just to stand at the fence. Looking at the pile of outdoor toys, Rascal chose a deflated football, which he began pushing around with his nose. The activity helped take

his mind off the frustration of being so close to home yet unable to complete his journey.

Of course, it would have been more fun if there were another dog to play with, but the shelter only let two dogs out together if they were positive that they would get along safely. Rascal grabbed the ball in his jaws and shook it from side to side. The ball flew away, and Rascal pounced after it. It landed right next to the fence, on the side where construction had begun for the new wing of the shelter. No workers were here now because of the bad weather.

As Rascal lunged for the ball like a hunter for its prey, his snout pushed it against the bottom of the fence and it wedged further underneath. One of the metal brackets that held the wire mesh to a post had come off – perhaps it had been knocked during the construction work. It meant that there was more give in the fence than usual, enough for the ball to make the fence bulge out at the bottom and create a slight gap.

Rascal looked down at it in curiosity. The question was – was it enough of a gap?

There was no time to find out. The door back into the shelter building opened and he heard the clang of a food tray, accompanied by a 'come here' whistle. There was no time for him to do anything. He padded back inside the building thoughtfully.

No doubt Rascal should have taken his time with the food in his bowl. After all, what was he going to do after he had eaten? But he had been hungry so often in the last few months that he couldn't stop himself from wolfing the food down at top speed.

He was just giving in to the usual after-meal drowsiness when the door to the dog section opened. As usual, the dogs at that end began to bark, and the barking spread from enclosure to enclosure like a wave.

'Be quiet, you lot!' said Lisa, then more quietly once the worst of the barking had died down, 'I'll just leave you to have a look around and get to know our dogs.'

The shuffle of feet indicated that there were a few other people with her.

'Thank you,' said a man's voice.

The door opened and shut again as Lisa left.

'Now remember, sweets,' said a woman's voice, 'we don't have to adopt a dog today, OK? We can come back lots of times until we find just the right one.'

'OK, Mum,' replied a girl's voice.

The footsteps grew louder and a moment later Rascal saw a young girl and her parents moving along the walkway between the two rows of enclosures. The girl went from cage to cage, giving each occupant a solemn look.

Rascal heard her reach the end of

the room and turn back. She stopped
again in front of the enclosure opposite
Rascal's, the one that held Toby, the little
Cocker Spaniel.

'I like this one,' the girl said. 'I like
those long, floppy ears!'

Her parents joined her. Toby lifted
his head with a whimper of hopeful
curiosity.

'It's not a puppy,'
said her dad.

'He's a *he*, not an
it,' corrected the
girl, pointing to
the card attached to

the front of the dog's enclosure. 'And he's eight.'

'It does say he's got a nice tempera-ment,' added the girl's mum.

'Let's just have a proper look at the others,' said her dad. 'Choosing a dog is an important decision. It's not the same as picking out a toy. This is like getting a new member of the family.'

But the girl wasn't listening. She had turned and was looking right at Rascal. 'No, wait,' she said. 'This is the one! Look at him! This is exactly the sort of dog I wanted.'

The girl's parents turned their attention

to Rascal. 'It says that this one isn't available for adoption,' said her mum.

'But he looks really nice!' said the girl. 'And smart, too! Look at his eyes!'

'He probably isn't available *yet*, that's all,' said her dad. 'I bet we'll be able to come back in a few days and he will be.'

Rascal lay and listened carefully as the family talked. He didn't understand everything that was said, of course, but he remembered enough about how this sort of place worked. You were here for what seemed like forever, but then — if you were one of the lucky ones — a family came and took you away from this place. The way this family was talking now reminded him of how the Holland family had adopted him from the shelter back when he was just a puppy.

But then he glimpsed Toby in the enclosure across the way. The Spaniel lay with his head on the ground, his sad eyes looking up at the family.

Rascal was not the kind of dog that would do anything to harm a human. He would never do anything to threaten a human. But there were times when you had to do something that truly went against your own nature and now was just such a time.

Rascal began to growl. He hated to do it, but he forced himself to carry on. It wasn't loud, just a low rumble in the dog's throat, but that made it all the more threatening. Despite the locked door between them, the man took a step back. Rascal let the growl build into a sharp bark. He told himself that he was Toby's only chance. The girl's eyes opened in alarm.

'I don't think this one would make a very good pet,' said her mother. Her husband shook his head in agreement.

It was only then that Rascal realised Lisa had rejoined the family.

The girl's father turned to her now. 'We'd like to know a little more about the spaniel,' he said.

'About Toby!' said the girl enthusiastically.

Lisa started to tell them all about what a friendly, good-natured dog Toby was, but before she did, she threw a worried

frown in Rascal's direction. Maybe the
police report was right. Maybe this dog
was a biter?

CHAPTER 8

Early the next morning, around the time he would usually be getting up, Joel was in the television studio.

'Ready in about ten minutes, OK?' said a man with headphones and a clipboard. Joel nodded and took another sip of water.

His excitement about being at the local television station was diminished by how early in the morning he'd had to get here. It had still been dark when he and his mum had set out in the car.

His mum fussed with his hair once again.

'It's fine, Mum,' he said, pulling his head away.

'Just relax and be yourself,' she added.

Joel nervously fingered the microphone that had been pinned to his sweater. He watched as the weatherman in the studio gave the local forecast for the next

few days. The man was standing in front of nothing but a big blue screen, but Joel saw on a monitor that it looked as if he was actually standing in front of a weather map.

'No snow this far west yet,' the weatherman said, 'but they've already had the first snowfall east of Woodford. And plenty more is expected – there'll be a winter storm warning in effect – and it's going to be heading our way. So make sure you dig out your snow boots!'

The station cut to advertisements. While they were off air, the producer led Joel to the desk where he would be interviewed. It was strange to meet the presenter, whose face Joel had seen so often on TV.

The presenter winked at Joel. 'It'll be over before you know it, kid,' he said.

And then the producer was counting down the seconds until they were back on air and Joel was suddenly aware of the huge TV camera trained on him.

'We've all heard stories about amazing pets,' said the presenter straight to the camera, 'but our next guest, Joel Holland, can top them all.' He turned to Joel. 'Tell us what happened when you were on holiday this last spring.'

Joel took a
deep breath
and began
to tell the
story of how
he and Rascal
had been parted in the caves all those
months ago. As he remembered that
terrible day, he forgot about the TV
camera.

'And you thought you'd lost him
forever?'

'I thought he was dead,' answered Joel.
Even though he'd told himself that he
wouldn't go all blubbery, tears stung his

eyes at the memory. He blinked them back.

'But months later you found out that Rascal *wasn't* dead,' prompted the presenter. 'Tell us how that happened.'

Joel explained how he had seen Rascal on a news report, how he had been sure it was the same dog. He gave the address of the website his mum had set up, and he held a photo of Rascal up to the camera. It showed the dog with a frisbee in his mouth, ready to play. Joel's fingers shook as he held the photo, but the cameraman still managed to get a good close-up.

And then the presenter was wishing him good luck and the interview was over.

'Is that it?' Joel asked, as his microphone was unclipped.

'That's it,' said the producer with a smile.

'Well, just one other thing,' she added. 'I know what it's like to lose a pet. I want to wish you the best of luck finding your dog! I really hope being on TV helps.'

Me too, thought Joel. *Me too.*

★ ★ ★

The last place Freddie had expected to be before the holidays was inside a hospital.

It was amazing to him that he didn't have more serious injuries. The doctor at the hospital said he'd suffered a bad concussion – he hadn't even woken for forty-eight hours (though apparently he'd sung a few rock songs in his sleep). He knew that he'd had a lucky escape in the crash. He had plenty of cuts and bruises, but nothing too serious.

Freddie had called his sister on the phone and explained that, all being well, he'd be able to leave the hospital the next day, after just a few more tests.

'It's a good thing you only hit your head,' she said, when she knew that he was going to be OK. 'You don't use it for much anyway, do you?'

'Ha, ha,' Freddie had replied, something he had said regularly to his big sister throughout their childhood.

With time to kill, he wandered to the TV room. Freddie had wanted to watch music clips, but the two other patients outvoted him. That was the only reason he ended up watching the morning news programme.

He kept half an eye on the news and

weather, idly flicking through one of the many out-of-date magazines on the coffee table.

He was vaguely aware that the presenter was talking to a boy on the programme now, something about a missing dog . . .

And then Freddie looked up and saw the photograph that filled the screen. He could hardly believe his eyes.

'Rocker!' he exclaimed. 'That dog's Rocker!'

One of the other patients had picked up the remote control and was aiming it at the TV.

'I want to find the basketball results,' he mumbled.

'No!' yelled Freddie. 'Don't change the channel!' He leaned forwards and listened intently as Joel Holland told the story

of Rascal the dog, also known as Rocker.

Five minutes later, Freddie was heading back to the telephone.

CHAPTER 9

In school, it was the last day of term – the last day of the whole school year – and there was a buzz of excitement in the air.

Joel's arrival halfway through the morning had only added to the excitement. Lots of kids in the school had seen him on TV that morning. Several told him that they had recorded it, in case Joel wanted to see what he looked like on screen. (In fact, Joel's big sister, Catherine, had recorded the segment too.) One or two kids took the opportunity to poke fun – pretending to cry and wailing 'Oh, my poor little doggy!' – but most were sympathetic and encouraging.

After lunch, Joel's teacher abandoned all pretence of getting any work done. He had allowed the class to bring in board games or books, and there was a hubbub of happy activity in the classroom.

Joel joined in a game, but it was impossible for him to concentrate. He kept wondering if anyone had called with information about Rascal. So when the intercom crackled, 'Joel Holland, please come to the school office,' he leapt up so quickly that he almost knocked the board game flying.

He made his way to the school office as fast as he could, without actually running in the corridors.

Joel was surprised to find his mum waiting for him.

'Get your coat,' she told him. 'You're leaving early.'

'What is it?' he asked. 'Is something the matter?'

His mum shook her head and smiled, but her eyes shone with tears. Joel thought he could hear anxiety in her voice.

'It's Rascal,' she said. 'I think we may have found where he is.'

Joel's heart didn't just jump, it did a triple somersault! Could this be true?

'Where?' he asked. He knew that a big stupid grin was plastered on his face and he didn't mind one little bit.

'We think he's in the animal shelter over in Marshall County,' she said.

Marshall! The town of Marshall wasn't far away from them at all! That meant that Rascal had almost completed his long journey home.

'Did you call them to make sure?' he asked,

trying to ignore the excited thudding of his heart.

'There's a bit of a problem. Some of the telephone lines are down around Marshall,' said his mum. 'It must be the winter storm blowing through. I kept trying but I could only get an automated message from the operator. But don't worry . . . Even in the bad weather, we can drive over there within an hour.'

Joel gave a vigorous nod of the head. 'So what are we waiting for?'

On the drive over, Joel's mum explained what she knew about the situation. As far as she could tell, Rascal had been in a vehicle that was involved in a crash on the highway.

'He wasn't hurt, was he?' asked Joel worriedly.

'No,' said Mum. 'Well, I don't think he was.'

She went on to tell how the man in the accident had been in a nearby hospital. He had tried already to find out what had happened to Rascal, and the local police department had promised to get back to him. But then he had seen Joel on the morning news and he had instantly recognised Rascal's photograph.

His next telephone call had begun a chain of hurried calls – to the Marshall police department, the television station and finally the Hollands' house. Piecing the information together like a jigsaw puzzle, Joel's mum realised that the police officer must have thought that Rascal had caused the accident. She knew that he had been taken to the shelter. But then she wasn't able to telephone the shelter to confirm this. Nor could the police send an officer over to the shelter – with a big storm on the way, they couldn't spare anyone until the next day at the very earliest. No, the easiest thing was for Joel and his mum just to drive there themselves.

The further east they went, the darker and darker the sky became with towering grey clouds. There was plenty of snow at the side of the highway here, but it looked as if the forecast had been right – there was a lot more on the way.

As Mum took the Marshall exit off the highway, the snow was beginning to fall, and by the time they reached the animal shelter, it was coming down heavily.

The woman at the front desk in the reception area wore a name badge that said BECCA on it. It looked brand new. She seemed flustered as she flicked through a stack of papers on the front desk.

'I'm sorry to keep you waiting,' she said at last to Joel and his mum. 'Things are a bit chaotic, I'm afraid. This is my first week working here – I'm not really meant to be here on my own but Lisa, the shelter director, hasn't made it in. She lives up over Middleton way and I think the roads there might be closed because of the storm. But I can't check because our phones aren't even working.' There was a note of panic in her voice.

Joel's mum explained that they had

been told that Rascal was here and she gave a quick description of the family pet.

Becca nodded quickly. 'Yes, I'm sure we've got a dog that fits that description. Come this way.'

They followed Becca to the dog area. The barks that erupted when the door opened were louder than ever, probably because their food was late in coming today.

Becca walked along to Rascal's enclosure . . . and froze. It was empty.

Frowning, Becca rushed along to the window at the end of the walkway and looked out to the dog runs outside. But they too were empty.

'I . . . don't understand,' said Becca.

A chill of unease ran down Joel's spine. Something was wrong.

'Perhaps he's been moved to another enclosure,' suggested Joel's mum. But it only took a minute or two to check that this wasn't the case.

Back at the front desk, Becca rifled through the shelter's paperwork.

'He hasn't been adopted by someone, has he?' asked Joel's mum.

'No, I'm sure he hasn't. I'd have a record of that right here . . .' Becca suddenly looked up, a look of pale horror on her face. 'Unless . . .'

'Yes?'

'The dog you're looking for, we were told he might be dangerous.'

Joel's mum nodded. 'Yes, that was just a misunderstanding. They thought that Rascal had caused the accident, but he didn't.'

But the grim look didn't leave Becca's face. 'Well he definitely hasn't been adopted. The only thing I can think is . . . They must have needed the space for another dog. I . . . I'm afraid he must have been put to sleep . . . I'm so sorry.'

She began to explain how the shelter hardly ever put dogs down, and on the few occasions they did, the method – an injection – was swift and painless. But Joel didn't hear the rest of the woman's explanation. He didn't notice his mum's arm around his shoulders. The terrible words echoed in his mind. Put to sleep! Only it wasn't *to sleep*, was it? His dog had been put down forever. It wasn't fair! Rascal had travelled such a great distance; he had battled almost the entire way home.

And now, after all that and with such a little way to go, Rascal was dead!

CHAPTER 10

There were so many ifs. If Becca hadn't
been new at the shelter . . . If the phones
had been working around Marshall . . .
If the storm hadn't prevented Lisa
from making it to the shelter as she
usually did . . . If any of these things had

happened, they would have been able to work out the truth of the matter right away.

In fact, Rascal was cold and he was hungry and tired . . . and he was very much alive.

When he had been let out into the dog run late that morning, he ran straight to the far side of the fence, where he found the broken section with the deflated football still wedged under the mesh. He drove it further in, and then he began to dig away at the earth with his front paws. The cold ground was hard, but once the top layer was gone, it became a little easier. At any moment, he expected a voice to shout at him, but none did.

At last, the gap beneath the fence seemed big enough for him to squeeze his head through. Then came the hard part. It seemed impossible that he would get his shoulders through as well. The sharp points of the bottom of the fence dug into him, but Rascal wriggled and crawled, dismissing the pain as the fence scraped along his back. He was making it! He thought that the worst might be over when he'd got his chest through, but he hadn't anticipated how much his damaged back leg would hurt when he pulled it through. The pain was terrible, but there was no way he could go back now. Stifling a howl of pain, he hauled himself through.

And then he was standing on the other side of the fence. The wind was bitter, but to Rascal at that moment it felt wonderful. He had done it! But he knew that he couldn't hang around here congratulating himself. He ran for the shelter of the trees ahead, and then on westward.

He was feeling well-rested and strong at first, but the cold in the air soon

sapped his energy. There was quite a lot
of snow on the ground. Soon the pads
of his feet were numb with the cold.

But on he ran. He wouldn't
let himself stop, not now,
when he was so

close to
home. When he
needed a drink he simply
bent his head to lap up snow.

At first Rascal followed the line of the
highway, before veering off to the hills
to one side. This route would cut a long
way off the rest of the journey. What
Rascal didn't know was that, even as he

was moving away from the highway, Joel
and his mum were joining the very same
road just a few miles to the east, on their
way to the shelter.

The dog battled on all afternoon. The
terrain was uneven and occasionally he
wandered into snowdrifts that he had
to push his way through. The going got
harder still as the snow fell more heavily.
As evening came, the snow did not
abate. Everything seemed bathed in a
cold, blue light, muffling all sounds
in the forest around him, so that he
began to feel like the loneliest creature
on the planet.

As the hours went by, Rascal's tiredness grew and grew until it blotted out almost every thought in his mind. The only one he could hold on to was the one that kept him going – home! Though his legs ached with weariness and were numb with cold, he knew that each step was taking him closer and closer to home.

It was more and more difficult to judge the snow's depth, and the blanket of white concealed various logs and bushes that tripped him. But whenever Rascal tumbled forwards into the snow, he pulled himself to his feet again.

It seemed as if the snow would keep falling forever, that this was what the entire world consisted of now – the night, the woods and the falling snow.

But eventually, it began to subside and then finally stop. And when it did, Rascal saw a wonderful sight in the distance below. It was the lights of a town – *his* town! One of those lights glittering below belonged to the house that was *his* home!

The sight gave him a fresh surge of energy. At last Rascal was at the foot of the hills and the ground under the snow was once again pavement. Now he trotted under the glare of street lights, running from one pool of orange light to the next. It was late by now, and he heard only a few cars in the distance. None passed him.

Part of Rascal's mind was insisting that he should just have a bit of a rest, but he knew that if he lay down now, he might not be able to get up again. His body was wracked with cold and pain.

But he was still able to lift his head and sniff the air. He was rewarded with a flood of familiar smells. He was close to his old neighbourhood. They gave him another tiny burst of energy.

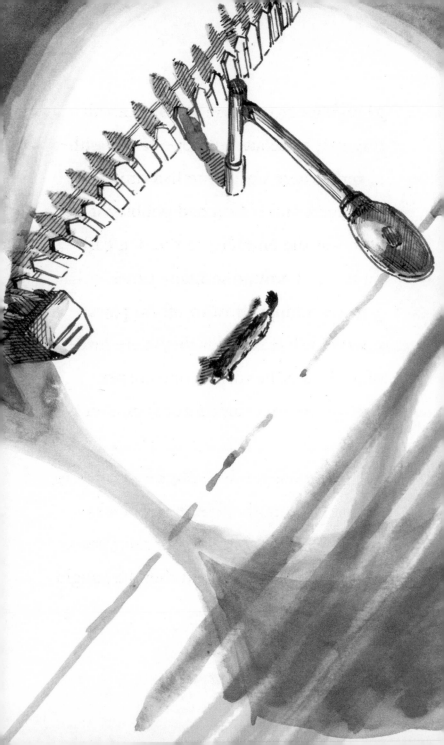

Memories crowded in as he made his way past place after place – here was the bakery where Catherine had dropped a doughnut and Rascal had gobbled it up; here was the entrance to the dog park he had run around so many times.

It was a huge effort to lift his paws now – his legs felt as if they were made of lead – but he turned one corner, crossed the street and turned another. He was nearly there. Rascal's walk had become a stagger now, but he just had to keep going another couple of blocks.

He heard the sound of running paws, muffled by the snow, and then he caught the scent of an old enemy. It was Fritz! Fritz the Dobermann, the dog who had delighted in chasing and bullying him ever since Rascal had been a puppy.

The big dog's owners usually let him out late at night. Fritz was often content to stay in the yard, but if something beyond the fence attracted his attention, he didn't have much difficulty getting out. The smell of another dog in the neighbourhood was more than enough to get Fritz going. As he raced towards Rascal now, he looked more like a guard dog than a pet.

Once there had been a time when

the very mention of Fritz's name would have caused Rascal to cower or run. Not any more. As the Dobermann raced towards him, Rascal held his ground, and it wasn't fatigue that stopped him from fleeing. He was a different dog now. He had survived constant hunger, treacherous rivers and raging fires. He had faced coyotes and dogs and snakes and he had faced people who hated strays like him, and he had survived them all. Fritz didn't seem like much of a problem in comparison.

When the big dog was almost upon him, Rascal let out a bark. It wasn't

especially loud, but somehow that bark
contained all of the frustration Rascal
had felt on his
long journey
home, and all
of the inner
strength that he
had built up, too, over those long, long
months.

Fritz pulled up fast, wagging his
stubby tail in nervous confusion. His
nose told him that he knew this dog, but
there was something about it that made
him uneasy. He gave a gruff little bark,
mostly for show, and then turned round

and ran back to his own house.

Rascal was exhausted. He tottered forwards. Chains of Christmas lights in a few houses lit the street. They seemed to dance and blur in front of Rascal's eyes. His head seemed to be spinning.

But the house was there, just up ahead. He could see it, could imagine the cosy smell of it, the look of every single room.

He took a final step, wobbled, and then collapsed.

CHAPTER 11

Mum and Joel had had to remain in Marshall for the rest of the evening because the snow had closed down a stretch of the highway. At first, they'd thought that they would have to stay in a motel, but it said on the radio that the storm would end fairly quickly. Once fresh snow stopped falling, the snowploughs would quickly make the highway accessible again.

And so it was late when they finally drove home. Joel was silent in the back seat, but Mum knew that he wasn't sleeping. She tried to think of something to say, anything that could comfort him, but the words would not come.

It was close to midnight when they turned off to the streets of Woodford. The smaller roads still hadn't been ploughed.

'I don't think I can get the car up our

street,' said Mum, when they came to the foot of the hill that they lived halfway up. 'I'll have to go the long way round.'

'Can I get out and walk?' asked Joel. These were the first words he'd said in over an hour.

The house was in sight from here and Mum knew that Dad and Catherine would be home and waiting up. She nodded.

The snow crunched under Joel's feet. He had no gloves or scarf on, and the cold air stung his hands and face, but he didn't care. He looked up at the night-time sky. The clouds had begun to part and, even amidst the glow of Christmas lights, he could make out a few stars. When he saw the solitary North Star, a sob escaped him. He could remember sitting outside with Rascal on many an evening, looking up at the stars, pointing out that one in particular.

He would never be able to do that again.

Suddenly he saw something up ahead, an animal. It was lying in the snow between the sidewalk and the street. A racoon, perhaps? Whatever it was, it wasn't moving. Was it dead? Joel slowed down, ready to go around the animal.

But then Joel realised that this wasn't a

racoon. It was a dog, and it wasn't just any old dog. He got closer and . . .

'Rascal?'

Was it a trick? Were his eyes just showing him the one thing in the world he most wanted to see? No, it was true! The dog was really here. Rascal was really here. Joel began to race forwards.

Meanwhile, Rascal's dreams were nothing but cold, a more terrible coldness than any he had ever known. He no longer had the energy to fight; he just let himself be carried by it, as if he were swept along on a sea of cold.

But then a voice drifted across that sea,

pulling him back.

'Rascal!'

How long had it been since he had heard that name? How long since he had heard that voice?

With effort Rascal's eyes slowly opened. He was still lying on the snow-covered ground, but someone was

kneeling over him.

It was Joel! Tears were streaming down the boy's face, tears of disbelief and happiness. Rascal let out a gentle bark, full of relief at being home, at being back where he was supposed to be. Back with Joel!

He had hoped for this moment for so

long that it hardly seemed real, but it *was* real, because then the boy was hugging Rascal and pressing his cheek into the side of the dog's neck, and Rascal was licking Joel's laughing face.

The two were still this way when Mum's car pulled into the driveway up ahead. They were still hugging and laughing when Dad and Catherine joined Mum at the front door to witness the amazing sight.

Finally, Joel stood up. Rascal got to his feet too, but Joel just smiled. Bending down he scooped the dog up, cradling him in both arms. 'You don't have to

make it on your own,' he said. 'Not now.'

Joel started towards the house. 'Let's go home together.'

Early the next morning, Rascal dreamed that his belly was full and he was in a lovely, warm place with the ones he loved and who loved him. When he half-opened his eyes he saw that it wasn't a dream at all. He *was* home – home! – and there was Joel, in his own bed with a look of contented peace on his sleeping face.

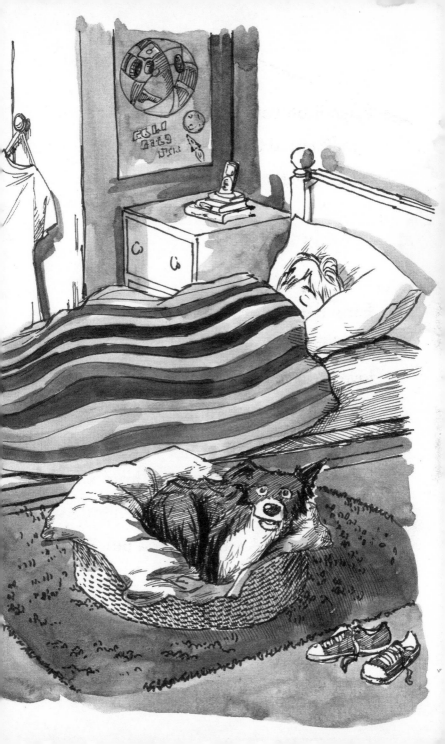

After all these months of weary loneliness, Rascal was back with his master. They would be able to run together through the park! If there was still enough snow on the ground, Joel might go sledding on the hill at the golf course and Rascal could charge after the sled as he always did! Or they could play catch with any of Rascal's wide assortment of tennis balls, frisbees and chewed-up toys!

The dog looked at the sleeping boy. There was so much they could do now they were together again, but there'd be plenty of time for all that. For now, it was hard to say no to just a little more rest after such a very long journey. Rascal flopped back down into his nice warm basket, right next to Joel's bed, and let sleep wrap its tender arms around him once again.